W9-BXD-519

LEPRECHAUN TALES

Also by Kathleen Green

PHILIP AND THE POOKA
AND OTHER IRISH FAIRY TALES

LEPRECHAUN
TALES

KATHLEEN GREEN

ILLUSTRATIONS BY

Victoria de Larrea

J · B · LIPPINCOTT COMPANY

Philadelphia   *New York*

Copyright © 1968 by Kathleen Green
All rights reserved
Library of Congress Catalog Card Number 68-10771
Printed in the United States of America
FIRST EDITION
Typography by Tere LoPrete

CONTENTS

❖ ❖ ❖

LEPRECHAUN TALES

❊

THE

LEPRECHAUN

AND THE

WHEELBARROW

———— ❀ ❀ ❀ ————

LUPREEN the Leprechaun was moving and he was in a bad temper about it. He'd been very comfortable under the old thorn tree on the hill. Very comfortable indeed! His home was snug in winter and airy in summer and he'd got it all fixed up with shelves for storing shoes and leather and nails. But it wasn't possible to stay on there, now that work had started again in the old stone quarry on the other side of the hill.

To be sure, the workers were still far from his tree

and might never actually reach it. But the noise they made! Their truck and their stone-breaker—to say nothing of their loud blasting. Leprechauns sleep during the daytime, and Lupreen had sometimes been hurled out of his bed when the explosions went off. Even a good-tempered leprechaun couldn't put up with that.

There was a nice thorn tree only two miles away. It wasn't as old and crooked as his own, but it would improve in time. He had been burrowing under it in secret for some time now and had his new house hollowed out and ready. And now all he had to do was to get on with the moving.

He had a lot of things to move. He had his bench, leather, nails, and *several* lasts, because the feet of the fairy people varied so much in size and shape. The odd shoes he'd made and mended in his time! When he thought of them he had to grin, even though he was in bad humor. Then, of course, there was his crock of gold, a good-sized, heavy iron pot almost full with gold dust, which the people of Tir na nOg had paid him for their shoes.

When the leprechaun had collected all his possessions they made a great heap in the center of his little room. He pushed back his green cap and scratched his head with a long, bony finger.

"Now, if I carry that piece by piece," he said to

himself, "I'll be nights and nights working at it. And I'll be footsore from walking. Two miles there and two miles back—to say nothing of the loss of trade and keeping my customers waiting. It's dangerous these days to let work pile up—too much competition. Bother that quarry anyway!"

He hopped round and round his heap of possessions, shaking his head until his long ears flapped and his long beard waggled.

"If I even had a wheelbarrow," he said, and stopped suddenly as the idea struck him.

The quarry! There must be plenty of barrows there, to judge by the sound of trundling and rumbling that was always going on. All right! The quarry people were putting him out of his home, so he would take a barrow for his moving. He'd put it back later, of course.

No sooner said than done. Lupreen loped off to the quarry. He could find only two wheelbarrows, but he took one of them and trundled it off to the thorn tree.

Then the loading began. Up and down he went between his little room and the open field. Up and down—staggering under the lasts and hammers and leather. It took much longer than he had expected, and by the time he had got the barrow loaded and the crock of gold safely wedged in between the other things so that it wouldn't fall off or spill, there was quite a lot of light in the sky and the birds were beginning to sing.

"Botheration!" said Lupreen. "I'll have to go ahead now. I simply couldn't *un*load again. But if anybody sees me—?" He shook his head as he lifted the handles of the barrow and began to trundle.

It was hard going. The ground was rough and the barrow heavy, and he couldn't take the shortest way, over ditches and fences, as he would have done without the load. He had to open gates and wheel his barrow through, and pull branches out of its way, and lift stones from under its wheels. Besides, there was *far* too much in the barrow. Something was always falling off—a half-made shoe or a packet of nails. By the time Lupreen had gone half a mile he was tired and cross, and the sun was beginning to get warm.

Now, fairy gold should not be allowed to get warm. It is different from ordinary gold, being gathered from sunsets and the wings of moths and the dust of the flowers in Tir na nOg. It should be kept cool under the roots of a thorn tree, not wheeled in a barrow through morning sunlight. When Lupreen stopped to mop his brow with his cap and peeped at his gold, he simply yelped with horror. The crock was full of yellow liquid, for all the world like melted butter!

Here was a nice thing! It would take all next winter to stiffen it, and then all his spare time for the next year to pound it with his hammer into dust again. Lupreen squeaked in rage and went jumping round the field in which the barrow was now standing.

"Botheration!" he yelped. "Those quarry people. Grrrrrrrr!"

But worse was to come. In his rage he didn't look where he was jumping, and down he came on a packet of nails that had just fallen out of the barrow. Of course, the nails stuck into his shoes. Luckily the soles were thick, but when Lupreen had tugged out all the nails the shoes were really in a very bad way.

A leprechaun simply must not walk in broken shoes. It is against the fairy law—it is against all the rules—and what is worse—it is *not done!* A leprechaun must mend his shoes the very minute they need it, and that is why one can hear them tap-tap-tapping in all sorts of odd places in the country. Lupreen had never been in such a hurry in his life. He *must* reach his new home before people were about. But yet—he had to take out his tools and start soling his shoes.

Tap-tap-tap. Tap-tap-tap, he went.

Now it happened that a tramp was fast asleep at the other end of the field, his head on his little bundle, his hat over his face.

Tap-tap-tap. The tramp stirred and opened his eyes. What was that? Or was it something he had dreamed? Tap-tap-TAP. He got up quietly and peered over the ditch, and then he rubbed the sleep from his eyes and had another look. A funny little old man in a green cap was just putting on his shoes. Beside him was a wheelbarrow loaded with all sorts of odds and ends. He must be a tinker, the tramp decided, or travelling odd-job man. Then the tramp saw the black iron pot on the barrow and wondered if there were anything in it that one could eat!

"Good morning to you," he said, bounding over the ditch.

The little man jumped about two feet off the ground and his face went white.

"You're up early, Daddy," said the tramp. "Or did you sleep here? I saw you putting on your shoes. Have you had breakfast yet, Daddy?"

Lupreen nearly choked as he tried to swallow his fear and his anger at being called "Daddy" by this dirty stranger.

"Not yet," he said. "Will you join me?" He dived into the wheelbarrow and pulled out a cake of his own homemade soda bread. How the tramp grabbed for it! And how he bit into it! As for Lupreen, he couldn't have touched a bite. He'd never been in such a fix before. Caught in broad daylight, with all his goods in a wheelbarrow.

"That's a fine bit of bread, Granda," said the tramp, who still had his eyes on the black iron pot. "What's in that?" And he walked over and looked in. "Butter—melted butter! Well, I never! You've let the sun melt your butter into oil, Granda dear. But it should taste all right—" and the tramp reached out with his piece of soda bread to dip it into the pot of melted gold!

Quick as a flash, Lupreen grabbed his hammer and hit the man sharply on the wrist. The tramp yelled and drew back.

"It's not butter—it's—it's oil for the wheelbarrow," cried Lupreen. "Ow—ow! Let go! Oh, my poor beard!"

"You little rascal," cried the tramp. "Just you try hitting me with a hammer again. I'll teach you some manners—Grandaddy. It's yourself that needs a bit of oiling and not the wheelbarrow."

And he seized Lupreen firmly and began to push his face into the pot of gold. The leprechaun squirmed and wriggled, but already his long beard was dipping deeply into the gold. And then—BOOM —the first explosion of the day came from the quarry!

Just for a second the tramp relaxed his grip, and in that second Lupreen had freed himself.

BOOM! There was another ear-splitting bang—

but it seemed to blast an idea into Lupreen's ringing head.

"Oh, sir," he wailed. "Don't be hard on me, sir. I'm only a little travelling cobbler, and you, who are so strong, are a King of the Roads. I must crawl like a snail with this heavy barrow—but you can travel like the wind, so light and free. Why, sir, you must have gathered the wisdom of the four provinces of Ireland!"

"Well, now, Grandaddy," said the tramp doubtfully, rubbing his head. "I've learned a thing or two, as you might say."

"Then you can see a good bargain when you come across it," said Lupreen quickly. "I'll give you a grand new pair of boots if you'll help me to push this barrow for about a mile. I want to camp for a bit in a field there. Listen, my lord, they'll be the best boots you ever had, and they'll never wear out."

Boots were one of the great problems of the tramp's life. He never had a pair that really fit—just castoffs—and as soon as they became comfortable and stopped pinching his corns, they were just about ready to throw away. Now, if this funny little man really made him a pair of new boots, it would be worth wheeling an old barrow for a mile or two.

"When do I get the boots?" he asked suspiciously.

"Before noon," Lupreen promised.

"Well, if I don't I'll wheel it back again, Grandaddy," said the tramp, and he seized the handles of the heavy barrow and set off at a good pace. He had wheeled it the mile in the time it would have taken Lupreen to make his way across one stony field.

Under the thorn tree, that was to be his new home, the leprechaun placed his precious pot in the shade, emptied the barrow, and set to work on the boots. He worked like lightning, and used his very best leather. And the tramp sat and rubbed his eyes, for the boots were growing before them just like magic—and, of course, it was magic. And when the boots were ready, just before noon, they were a perfect fit, and the nicest boots he had ever seen. Fit, indeed, for a King of the Roads, he told himself proudly as he laced them up.

"Indeed, I've got the best of the bargain," he said. "If there's anything else I can do for you before I go, Grandaddy, just say so."

"Will you take away this wheelbarrow," said Lupreen, who never wanted to see a wheelbarrow again as long as he lived. "I borrowed it from the stone quarry where the blasting was. Will you leave it back, someplace near the quarry, where they'll find it?"

But the tramp was suspicious again. If the little man were really a travelling cobbler he'd have his own barrow—and if it were not his barrow, what was he doing with a pot of oil for it? There was something funny going on, and he intended to stay and find out what it was all about. He wasn't going to walk off—certainly not!

But he was wrong! Just at that moment the fairy boots decided to walk off down the field, and as the tramp was in the boots he couldn't help going, too.

"Hi, Grandaddy!" he yelled.

"And stop calling me that!" screamed Lupreen, his rage finally getting the better of him. But now it didn't matter—for the tramp had his back to the leprechaun as he marched off in the magic boots, and once you take your eyes off a leprechaun you'll never see him again. In a split second, Lupreen had tipped all his possessions down into his hole, dived in, and banged his door shut. And because the door was covered with grass sods nobody would ever have found it.

When the tramp got the better of his feet and managed to come back, there was nothing but an empty wheelbarrow to be seen.

"Well, I never!" he said. "I should have guessed that little fellow was a leprechaun. Well, a bargain is a bargain—" and he trundled the wheelbarrow back to the field above the quarry, and went off to tell everybody he met about his adventure.

But nobody believed him—and nobody ever did believe him, even when he showed his boots and explained that no matter how far he walked they never needed to be mended and never wore out!

As for Lupreen—he had to cut off his beard, which was wet and sticky with gold, and put it away carefully to dry. Without it, he was the laughingstock of his customers, and he made up his mind that if he should ever have to change house again—even in a few hundred years time—he would carry his possessions one by one, and do all his moving under the cover of darkness.

TERENCE
THE TAILOR'S
JACKET

❀ ❀ ❀

It is many years since Terence the Tailor lived in the townland of Dunmalachi, but the people there still have a saying about anybody who needs a new suit of clothes.

"He's as shabby as Terence the Tailor," they say.

Certainly Terence wasn't a good advertisement for his own work. His elbows nearly always showed through his jacket, and the knees of his trousers could have done with a patch or two. But he was a very good tailor, was Terence, and when the Widow McNally, who lived in the cottage next to his, used to urge him to make himself a new suit he would always say—

"Haven't got the time, ma'am. Mustn't keep the customers waiting, ma'am, and I have orders that must be carried out without delay."

One would not have thought that in a place as small and poor as Dunmalachi there would have been so many orders for clothes! But there was Terence, snipping, stitching, chalking, and pressing, day in and day out. And the reason for this was that unknown to anybody, Terence, and his father before him, and his grandfather before that, had made clothes for some very shy customers who never came for fittings. These were the Lordly Ones, the people of the Sidhe who lived in the Fort, who sent their measurements and their beautiful bales of magically woven cloth to Terence, at dead of night in charge of a leprechaun or some other common type of fairy person.

They paid well, in gold dust, and Terence was making a nice little fortune.

Well, one evening he was hard at work on a cloak for one of the Lordly Ones when the Widow Mc-Nally started to beat on a tin tray out in the garden, to scare the birds away from her seeds. Such a noise she made! Terence went angrily to the window.

"Will you quit making such a din, ma'am?" he shouted. "Can't we have a bit of peace here?"

"That's all very well," said the Widow McNally,

and gave her tray another unmerciful bang. "But what about my seeds, to say nothing about the fruit that the creatures have eaten? It's grand to hear a blackbird whistling on a fine evening—especially if you know he's full to the very beak with red currants, huh!" And bang went the tray again.

"Can't you hang up something to scare them away?" cried Terence. "I'm at a most important order, and I'll cut it all wrong if that shocking noise goes on all evening. Why don't you make a scarecrow, ma'am?"

The Widow McNally put her head on one side. "Maybe I could do that," she admitted. "Maybe so, indeed. But I've nothing to put on it, unless you'd give me that ragged old jacket of yours. It's time, and more than time, that you made yourself a decent coat."

"It's not such a bad jacket," said Terence crossly.

"Give it to me for my scarecrow, or I'll bang this tray all evening, and every evening—and in the mornings, too," said the Widow McNally. "Sure you look like a scarecrow yourself, so you do."

Terence had to give in eventually, and promised to give her the jacket as soon as he had another one made for himself. Then he went back to his work on the cloak, and just then he got an idea.

The cloak was to be cut from a piece of the most

beautiful, fine, deep blue cloth—but if he cut it very carefully, and didn't make it as wide and luxurious as usual, he could save enough material to make himself a jacket that would make the people of Dunmalachi stare in envy when they saw it! It wasn't an honest idea, but Terence suddenly got such a longing for a blue jacket that he simply didn't care.

He made the cloak as skimpy as he dared, and when a leprechaun called for it that night at midnight Terence took his gold, and gave the parcel to the little fellow, without saying a word. Then, late and all as it was, he started work on his new jacket.

"So I look like a scarecrow, do I!" he muttered angrily.

By the next evening he had it finished, and then went out and helped the Widow McNally to make a fine scarecrow with two old broom handles and his old ragged jacket.

"And now, let's see you in your style!" commanded the Widow McNally.

Terence rolled down his shirt sleeves and went indoors to put on his new jacket. And there he got the most awful shock. The jacket sleeves were set in upside-down! At first he couldn't believe it, and then he went to the door again.

"You'll see it on me tomorrow, ma'am, when I'm

going down to the meeting in Dunmalachi in the evening," he called out to the Widow McNally.

Terence was simply furious that he could have made such a mistake, and before he went to bed that night he had ripped the sleeves out and put them in again right side up. But in the morning the same thing had happened, and this time Terence knew that he was being punished for having cheated his fairy customer.

"Well, maybe I can get it on as it is," he told himself, and he struggled into the coat.

It wasn't easy. The shoulder-pads were under his armpits, and when he moved his arms the strain on the cloth dragged the collar away from his neck. But he hadn't anything else to wear. It had rained during the night, and his coat flapped dismally on the Widow's scarecrow.

"It's all the Widow McNally's fault," grumbled Terence, most unjustly. "Well, anyway, her scarecrow doesn't seem to be much good."

And alas, that was so, for the birds were not one bit afraid. In fact, one of them was perched on Terence's coat, doing sentry for the others.

There was a very important meeting that evening. The men of Dunmalachi were coming together to decide to send a protest to the authorities who wanted to lay a new road. The fairy Fort lay in the track of the new road, and the people had no intention of seeing it destroyed.

Terence had to go to the meeting, of course, and when he set off the Widow McNally was at her gate to see his new jacket.

"It's a lovely bit of cloth," she admitted. "But how in the world did you come to make it so badly? It's not a fit at all!"

"It's a new style," said Terence, shoving his hands into his trousers pockets, because the shoulder pads seemed to be trying to push his arms up into the air. "It's so seldom I have anything new, I might as well give the people something to look at."

"They'll have that all right," said the Widow Mc-Nally with a chuckle.

Terence couldn't think of an answer so he waved good-bye to her and set off down the road. The trouble was that once his arm was up in the air and waving, he had the greatest difficulty in getting it down again. But he managed it, with a struggle, and got to the meeting without further bother.

The people of Dunmalachi were all very excited about the danger to the Fort—too excited to give Terence more than a glance. He managed to slip into a seat in the schoolroom, where the meeting was being held, and there he sat on his hands to keep the magical jacket from forcing his arms up into the air, because that was what it seemed determined to do.

The blacksmith was addressing the meeting, and as the whole gathering was agreed about the matter of the new road, they were able to get very worked up without any quarreling.

"So we're all agreed," shouted the blacksmith. "Our Fort must not be disturbed! Do you want to say something?" he added, glaring at Terence, because one of the poor tailor's hands had escaped and was waving about above his head.

"No! Oh, no!" cried Terence, going red, and succeeding in getting his hand under him again.

"Does anybody disagree?" yelled the blacksmith. "Because if anybody *does* I'm ready to change his mind for him—with these!" and he held up his great fists.

And now the jacket simply wrenched Terence's hands up, and began to wave them both about in the air like mad.

"So you want to fight me, do you, you little scrap of a tailor?" yelled the blacksmith. "Come on then!"

Terence didn't want to come on at all, but some of the excited crowd pushed him forward.

"I don't want the Fort to be harmed either," cried the poor tailor. But he was too late with his protests because the blacksmith had rushed at him.

Terence the Tailor's Jacket

Now Terence might be a small man, but he was tough, and he should have been able to put up a good enough fight. But the sleeves of the coat were behaving even worse than before. All Terence's punches went up into the air, and all the blacksmith's landed neatly, so that the tailor got a sound thrashing, and was thrown out into the street while the people jeered and booed after him.

It was a very sad Terence who limped his way home that evening, with the blue jacket hung over his arm. It was dark as he went past the Widow McNally's garden, and there—how nice and homely it looked—there hung his old jacket on the scarecrow. Terence stopped. If the old jacket were dried and brushed it couldn't look so very much worse than it had always done! And he could put his new one, which had caused him such disgrace, to scare the birds from the Widow's garden.

Next morning, when the Widow McNally looked out of the window, she thought she was still dreaming. For the scarecrow, in its blue jacket, was behaving as if it were alive, and waving its arms wildly above its head. The birds simply couldn't understand it either, and when the day wore on, and the scarecrow didn't seem to grow tired, they decided to go off and feed somewhere else.

Nor did they come back, because the scarecrow

kept waving, non-stop, day and night. The Widow was simply delighted, and no wonder, for the fairy material from which the coat was made seemed to take no hurt from the weather. It lasted for twenty years before it began to get ragged.

Terence got no further orders from the Lordly Ones for over a year, and he was afraid that the scare about the Fort had driven them away. But the Fort was saved by the protest meeting, and finally one night the messenger leprechaun appeared again with cloth and an order for a cloak.

Needless to say, the tailor was most honest this time, and begged the leprechaun to tell the noble people of the Sidhe how sorry he was. And the Lordly Ones, being really noble people, sent him so much work that he was busier than ever, and never got time to make himself a new jacket at all.

That is how the old saying started—"As shabby as Terence the Tailor." And they have another saying in Dunmalachi as well. When anybody gets a really fine outfit of clothes the people say: "Aye, he's all dressed up like the Widow McNally's scarecrow!"

THE PIPER WHO

COULD NOT PLAY

—— ❀ ❀ ❀ ——

As long as anybody could remember, and as far back as the old tales went, there had always been a piper in the little gray stone house at the crossroads. Who the first piper was nobody knew, but the pipes had been handed down from father to son ever since, and the people never lacked music when they gathered on the summer evenings at the crossroads to dance.

Peader was the son of the piper. He could play the mouth organ, the tin whistle, the melodeon, or indeed anything in the way of a musical instrument, and people said that when his turn came he would be the best piper that ever piped.

There had been a very severe winter, and the old

piper had coughed and sneezed and snivelled and wheezed until he had no breath left. When the weather began to get warm enough for the dancers to gather, the old man told Peader that he must play the pipes from that day on.

"Take good care of these pipes," he said. "They were specially made for your great-great-great-grandfather, by a strange man whom they called the Ceoltoir. He was half fairy and half man, so I've heard tell, and he made instruments for the people of the Sidhe. He put the most wonderful voice into our pipes."

So Peader took the pipes and began to play, and the noises that came out were so dreadful that the old man screamed for him to stop.

"Watch what you're doing, you fool," he cried. "Sure the wheeze that I have in my chest has a sweeter sound than that."

Peader took the pipes into a corner and sat down with them. He coaxed them, and stroked them, and breathed as gently as he knew how, and his father put his hands over his ears and stamped with his feet on the hearth.

"Will you stop," he cried. "I'd rather listen to a crow! I'd rather listen to my little Mouseen that has her hole behind the dresser, so I would. Go out to the turf shed until you've learned to play."

So Peader went out to the turf shed, but the pipes didn't sing any sweeter for him out there. Then some of the boys and girls that were gathered for the dancing came and found him.

"Your father says he's not playing the pipes anymore," they said. "Come on, Peader, and play for the dancing."

They dragged him out to the crossroads, shouting to the others, "Here's our new piper. Welcome to our new piper!"

Poor Peader. He simply didn't know what to do. "There's something the matter with the pipes," he said. "I'll play the mouth organ."

But they wouldn't have that at all. "The pipes, lad, the pipes," they shouted. Peader blew until he was red in the face, and the noise was so dreadful that all the dogs in the neighborhood began to howl, and the dancers gave up trying to dance and went home. Peader went sadly into the kitchen.

"A banshee would be ashamed to make the sound that you bring out of those pipes," said his father. "And you're the son of a piper and the grandson of a piper and the great-grandson of a piper. Shame on you! If you can't play you'd better go off and try to find the Ceoltoir that made them, and see if he can teach you how to play them. I've heard that he's still alive, although he must be close on two hundred

years old. That comes of being half fairy. They say he lives in a valley in the hills. It's called Halfway, because it's half in our world and half in Tir na nOg."

"That would be a shocking long journey," protested Peader. "Maybe if I practice for a few days—"

"Not if I can stop you," cried the old piper. "You'd drive me demented, and sure poor Mouseen is sulking in her hole, and hasn't come out for her supper since you started your screaming and squawking. Off with you!"

So the next morning Peader set off for the hills with the pipes slung on his back. He walked all day, and as the evening came on he sat down to rest himself, and had another try at the pipes. But so dreadful was the sound that he made that the curlew flew screaming into the air, and the sheep stampeded and went scurrying away down the hillside.

"What are you trying to do, boy?" said a voice, and Peader looked up and saw a little old man with the longest beard that he had ever seen, so long indeed that it hung well below his knees. He had a fiddle and bow under his arm, and Peader sprang to his feet and lifted his cap.

"Would you be the Ceoltoir?" he asked eagerly.

"I would not!" said the old man. "But I've travelled all day from the hills coming to see that same Ceol-

toir, for I'm in a bit of trouble with my fiddle-playing. I'm Lochrie the Fiddler."

"What's wrong with your fiddle?" asked Peader.

Lochrie sighed. "It's not my fiddle that's wrong, but my beard," he explained. "It's all right if there's no breeze, but the people insist on dancing in the open, round the thorn trees, and then if a bit of wind comes up I'm simply ruined. My beard blows down over the fiddle. It goes down the holes in the fiddle and stops the sound coming out. It gets tangled up with my fingers and bow and stops them moving. It makes me feel terribly foolish!"

"Why don't you cut your beard?" asked Peader.

"The Ceoltoir won't ask me a silly question like that," said Lochrie. "I belong to the clan of the Long Beards. I simply can't cut it. It would grow again overnight."

"I beg your pardon," said Peader. "I didn't know about that. But if you're going to the Ceoltoir may I go with you, for I don't know the way?"

"We're here already," said the little old man. "It's halfway, you know, halfway between your country and mine, so as we've both been travelling all day we must have arrived. I believe that he lives in that little hut over there. You must be careful what you say to him, lad, for he's very short-tempered, especially with people from your country."

"Maybe you would speak for me then, sir," begged Peader, as they drew near to the hut which was built of blocks of granite.

"Ceoltoir, noble Ceoltoir," cried Lochrie the Fiddler, tapping at the great thick wooden door. "Open your door and help two troubled musicians."

And at that the door opened and the Ceoltoir stood before them. He was very tall, and wore a long black cloak right down to his feet. He had the whitest face and hair that Peader had ever seen, and his eyes were black and piercing. As he brought them into the hut they could see that it was filled with all sorts of musical instruments. A black cat was sitting on the hearth and arched her back at them.

"What can I do for you, Lochrie the Fiddler?" asked the Ceoltoir, in a very deep voice, not even looking at Peader.

The little old man explained his problem, and the Ceoltoir laughed loudly. "My dear friend, that is easy," he cried. "Put up your fiddle under your chin. Now, bring your beard forward and under the instrument—so? Now, up and round the tuning pegs at the end—so! Tie it firmly. Now, where's your trouble, Lochrie? And not only is your beard safely out of the way, it will keep your pegs from slipping, and keep your fiddle in tune."

"But that's wonderful," cried Lochrie. "Why did I

never think of that? Here is your piece of gold, good Ceoltoir."

The Ceoltoir took the gold and put it in a great chest in the corner.

"This young piper is in trouble, too," said the Fiddler. "His pipes won't sing for him, and they're good pipes, your own make, too!

And at that Peader, who had his pipes ready under his arm, began to play.

"Stop," yelled the Ceoltoir, sticking his fingers into his ears. Indeed the sound was so horrible that Lochrie would have dropped his fiddle had not his beard held it fast; and the black cat began to stalk across the hut with every whisker bristling.

"What can I do?" asked poor Peader. "What's wrong with the pipes?"

"Nothing can ever go wrong with those pipes," thundered the Ceoltoir. "I made them. They are perfect. But you—you simply can't play them, and nobody can teach you. Go away, and learn to plough. If the pipes won't sing for you nobody can make you into a piper. Go!"

Lochrie the Fiddler caught poor Peader's arm and hurried him out. "What am I to do?" wailed Peader. "There's always been a piper at the crossroads."

"Take your pipes home," advised Lochrie. "Maybe

they're under a spell. I'd travel with you only that I've a dance to play for this very night. Hurry, for it's getting dark. Good-bye."

And the kind old man went dancing up the hillside fiddling the sweetest little jig that Peader had ever heard.

Poor Peader had a horrible journey home. He lost his way several times in the dark, and he could not help feeling that something was following him, although he could see nothing. At daybreak he was still far from home; and it was evening, and he was tired and hot, when he reached the crossroads, and saw, alas, that the dancers were gathering.

"Well?" said the old piper, as his son slunk shamefaced into the kitchen. "But what—what?"

At that moment the Ceoltoir's black cat, which had followed Peader all the way home, sprang with a howl on to the pipes. And at that very same instant a tiny mouse shot out through one of the holes and whisked under the dresser.

"Mouseen!" cried the old piper. "My little Mouseen. I thought you were dead on me, so I did, Mouseen! What did you want to take my pet mouse away with you for, you fool!" he shouted at his son.

"And to take my cat!" thundered the voice of the Ceoltoir from the doorway. "As if it wasn't enough that you offered me no money for my advice, you must take my cat away as well!"

"You advised me to learn ploughing," cried Peader. "Well, listen," and now that Mouseen was no longer in the pipes they began to sing and drone most sweetly. "What was your advice worth?" said Peader and stepped outside, playing the jig that he had heard Lochrie play on the fiddle.

"Well," said the Ceoltoir. "Well, perhaps I was a bit hasty. Hum-um-um, we'll say no more about paying. It's a pleasure to me if I have helped—"

"Listen," said the old piper. "Will you take that cat away! I want to coax Mouseen out and give her some supper, poor wee thing."

The Ceoltoir caught up his cat and stalked away, snorting with rage. "That's what comes of meddling with these *humans*," he snorted. "Nothing but insults. I'll not even stay halfway between the two worlds. I'll go right into Tir na nOg!" and he must have done so because he was never seen or heard of again.

But the pipes that the Ceoltoir had made are still singing at the crossroads. They say that Peader the Piper is better even than his father, or grandfather or great-grandfather. But then—they say—the fairies must have taught him, or that strange man in the black cloak that was seen that evening carrying the black cat. Remember how shockingly he played before! Yes, there's magic in it!

Peader knows what they say, but he has never told them about Mouseen. He just smiles to himself and swings into his finest jig, the one he learned from Lochrie the Fiddler.

GEORGE AND THE

FIELD GLASSES

———— ❈ ❈ ❈ ————

THERE is not a doubt in the world that old George was one of the most inquisitive people who ever lived. He could not bear to miss seeing anything, and it was his habit to go up to the flat roof of his house with a pair of field glasses, so that he could watch all his neighbors and keep an eye on the surrounding hills as well.

Naturally, he was not very popular, but after a time the neighbors got used to being watched and they put up with it and even made jokes about it, because no matter how much George spied on them he never gossiped about what he saw, and so there was no trouble.

But it so happened one day that George turned his glasses on a distant hillside, and there he saw a little

old leprechaun with long ears who was very busy
burying something in a hole that he had dug.

"Gold!" said George to himself. "As sure as eggs
are eggs he's burying his crock of gold! And look
how nicely he's fixing the stones over the loose soil
so that nobody would ever know it had been shifted.
Clever little fellow!"

And at just that moment the leprechaun, who *was*
a clever fellow, got a funny feeling all the way up his
back and knew that he was being watched. He
looked around, and saw in the distance George's field
glasses shining in the sunshine, like two curious
eyes.

The leprechaun was simply furious. He danced
about with rage until his long ears flapped, and
shook his fist towards George's house. Now he would
have to dig up his gold again, and bury it somewhere
else. After all his trouble, too! And he began to kick
at the stones he had gathered, and hurt his toes so
badly that he was just beside himself with rage.

"I'll put a spell on him, so I will," he panted, and
when he had finally pulled his crock out of the earth
again he took a pinch of gold dust between his finger
and thumb and blew it into the air, which was his
way of making magic.

"If you're looking through those glasses, Mister
Nosey George, when I happen to snap my fingers,"

said the leprechaum, "may the thing you are looking at turn into something dreadful!"

And then the leprechaun put his crock under his
arm and hopped off over the hilltop, out of sight.

Well, George hadn't intended to steal the leprechaun's gold anyway, and he was rather upset that
the little man had taken the trouble to dig it up
again.

"I was just *looking* at him," he said to himself, and
he turned away from the hillside and began to look
down into the next-door garden instead. Now two
old spinsters lived next door to George. They were
called Kate and Nora, and Kate had just come into
the garden with a basket of freshly washed clothes.

George adjusted his glasses and watched with in-
terest.

"Three aprons instead of two," he muttered. "One
of them must have spilled something on herself.
There's a split in that pillowcase; wonder they don't
mend it! Now that's a really nice lace handkerchief—"

And just as he was looking at the handkerchief
something happened. The long-eared leprechaun,
who was lying in the soft grass about two miles
away, lifted his hand and snapped his fingers. And
before George's very eyes the handkerchief turned
into a large, ragged tablecloth. And it wasn't a clean

one either. It was stained with ink and tea, and spotted with grease.

George nearly dropped his field glasses, but before he could recover himself, Kate, who had stooped to lift some more clothes from her basket, straightened up and saw the tablecloth.

"Sakes alive!" screamed Kate. "Who in the world has put that horrible thing on our line?" And then, because she more or less took it for granted that George was watching her, she looked up at his roof.

"I say, George," she shouted. "Did you see which of the boys climbed over the wall and put this cloth here? He must have been as quick as a flash about it!"

"Nobody put it there," called George. "There wasn't anybody in the garden at all! I was watching carefully."

"Indeed, I'm sure you were," snapped Kate. "But somebody *must* have come over the wall. You don't think we own this horrible thing, I hope!" And she took down the cloth in the tips of her fingers, threw it in the dustbin, and washed her hands.

It took George some time to recover himself from the shock he had had, but then he noticed that Nora was dusting the old china in the parlor. He could not resist turning his field glasses on the window to watch her. She had just dusted a lovely blue willow-pattern cup and put it down on a table while she turned to reach a teapot from her china cupboard.

George was still looking at the cup when the leprechaun, who had just lit up his clay pipe and taken a contented puff, held up his hand and snapped his fingers.

Well, when poor Nora turned round she just let her lovely teapot fall with a crash, for on the table was a huge, dirty coal scuttle, with dents in the sides and a hole in the bottom.

"Oh, dear, oh, dear," wailed Nora. "Someone has played a nasty joke on me and I've broken my nicest teapot. Kate, Kate, come here, and look at this horrible thing on our polished table!"

Meanwhile, up on his roof, George had had to put down his field glasses for a minute so that he could mop his brow.

"This is very strange, indeed," he said to himself. "It must have been that leprechaun. He was certainly very angry, and he's put a spell on the town, so he has!" And George took up the glasses again, and began looking to see if the leprechaun were anywhere about. "I must warn Nora and Kate," George said.

And just then the old women came into their garden together.

"Listen, George," shouted Nora. "You were watching, so you must tell us who is playing these pranks, and we'll go and complain."

"I didn't see anybody," George said. "There wasn't anybody to see!"

"How can you expect us to believe that?" screamed Kate. "We've put up with your spying for years, and this is all the thanks we get. Do you expect us to believe that *Tibby* has pinned a horrible old rag on our line and put a horrible old coal scuttle in our parlor?"

Tibby was their striped cat who was sitting in the sunshine washing his face just as George turned his glasses to look at him. And, far away, the leprechaun let out a neat smoke ring and snapped his fingers in the middle of it.

Well! When Tibby turned into a tiger everybody got the most frightful shock. George got the least, because he was beginning to expect magic—and besides, he was on the roof! Nora and Kate nearly fainted with terror, but poor Tibby got the worst shock of all. To see a tiger was bad enough, but to *be* a tiger was just too much for him. He let out the most dreadful roar, sprang over the garden wall, and went bounding away down the road towards the open countryside.

What a fuss there was! They called the police and

roused the townspeople, and everybody collected shotguns and sticks and went tiger hunting. Old George, on his roof with his field glasses, thought that he should be directing the hunt until, before everybody's eyes, a tiny weed in the middle of the market square turned into a huge monkey-puzzle tree. George had just been scanning the square, and the people turned indignantly on him.

"You're at the bottom of all this," they yelled. "You've let a tiger loose, and you've put this thing here just to give us the trouble of cutting it down. You've developed the Evil Eye, through all your spying!"

"Yes, just wait until we've caught this tiger, and then see what we'll have to say to you!" they threatened.

Poor George! How anxiously he scanned the countryside all that evening! Very fortunately the leprechaun had dropped off to sleep. Otherwise George might have produced horrors of all kinds. But by evening there was no sign of the tiger, and the hunt was called off until daybreak.

The next morning, just as it was getting light, George slipped out of his house and away into the hills. Firstly, he wanted to avoid the townspeople, and secondly, he wanted to see if he could find the

leprechaun. And if he should meet the tiger, well—
he didn't think a tiger would be any worse than his
neighbors at this stage.

Luck was with him, and before he had walked for
more than an hour his roving field glasses picked out
the little figure of the leprechaun fast asleep in the
grass.

"Ah," said George. "I'll wake him and beg his pardon," but at that very minute the leprechaun woke,
yawned, and—snapped his fingers!

Well, it was just too bad for the leprechaun that
George was looking at him through the field glasses
for now the little fellow was caught in his own spell.
Before George's horrified eyes the leprechaun's long
ears grew and grew and grew, until there were yards
and yards of long thin ear falling about him. He
whimpered and screamed and struggled, and before
he knew what was happening he was simply tied up
and helpless by his own ears. And at this minute
George was so weak with fright that he dropped his
field glasses, and smashed them to pieces.

"Help, help," yelled the leprechaun, and George
came closer carefully.

"Serves you right," he said. "Look at the things you
did to me, and I wouldn't have touched your gold.
I'm no thief, even if I am a bit too curious!"

"Listen," wailed the leprechaun, writhing about

and getting more tangled up than ever. "I must get to my crock of gold to make a counter-spell to get rid of these ears. Please untie me, good George!"

"If I help you, will you help me?" said George. "You could surely make the people stop hating me. And what about that tiger, you can't leave him wandering around."

"All right," cried the leprechaun. "Please help me!"

So George set to work, and he had a dreadful job, worse than unravelling a skein of wool. But when he got one ear free, and rolled it up, for all the world like a roll of hose pipe, the second one wasn't so bad. He gave them to the leprechaun to hold, one under each arm, and away hopped the little fellow to the bushes where he had hidden his crock of gold.

Puff, he went with a pinch of gold dust, and his ears were back to normal. Puff, he went, and poor Tibby, wandering unhappily in the hills, found that he was a striped cat again, and ran for home. Puff, and now the townspeople were waking up and thought, each one of them, that the whole thing was a dream. Puff, went the leprechaun, and blew himself right out of sight with his precious crock.

Only a few things were not quite normal. Nora and Kate were still short of one cup and one handkerchief, and still believed a joke had been played on them.

George had no field glasses, but that didn't matter, for he was completely cured of his curiosity.

And—there was still a monkey-puzzle tree in the middle of the market square. And nobody knew how it came to be there.

THE SALMON'S

REVENGE

———— ❀ ❀ ❀ ————

EVERYBODY knows the story of how the young Finn
McCool was sent by his teacher to cook the Salmon
of Knowledge, and how in cooking it he burned his
thumb, sucked it, and therefore was the first to taste
the fish, and became very wise. But what people do
not know is that the Salmon of Knowledge had a
brother, who was as wise as himself, because they
had always shared their wisdom, and a good deal
wiser—because the Salmon of Knowledge was
caught and cooked, whereas his brother is still alive
to this day. He lies in a very deep pool under shading
trees, in the part of his favorite river where it flows
through a stretch of woodland.

Tadhg the Poacher loved that part of the river,
too, and one fine night the Salmon swam up from his

bed in the mud to take some exercise, and the next minute he found himself struggling in the poacher's net.

Naturally, Tadhg knew nothing about the brother of the Salmon of Knowledge. He only knew that this great fat fish was something for a poacher to dream about.

"Oh, boys-a-boys, he's a whopper!" gasped Tadhg, as he pulled the net in close to the bank and reached for his gaff to kill the fish.

"Don't kill me! Let me talk to you!" cried the Salmon in a thin, whispering voice.

Tadhg nearly dropped his gaff, and looked about him, thinking that somebody was hiding in the trees behind him—perhaps a water bailiff!

"Listen to me," hissed the Salmon. "*Why* do you want to kill me?"

Tadhg began to shake all over. The voice was certainly coming from the net, but that could only mean that he, Tadhg the Poacher, was very seriously ill indeed, raving in fact. Fish *didn't* talk.

"*Why* do you want to kill me?" insisted the Salmon.

"Well, I want money, and you'll fetch a good price," said Tadhg, gaining courage.

"But your money will be gone in a few days," said the Salmon.

"You never said a truer word!" agreed Tadhg. "Money goes like water these days."

"I can teach you how to change your money into something better," said the Salmon. "But mind, this spell will only work with Irish coins, because I have only power over the world of fishes, birds, and animals. When you get a coin, Poacher, turn it over on your palm—"

"Sure I always do," interrupted Tadhg.

"Turn it three times," finished the Salmon firmly, "put it back in your pocket, and see what happens. Try the spell now, and see what value you get. Then make good use of it, for the power will not last for very long. Try it now!"

Tadhg had decided that he was fast asleep and dreaming, but it was a fine dream. He fumbled in his pocket and found a penny, an Irish one with a hen on it. He laid down his gaff, turned the penny three times, and shoved it in his pocket. The next second a live hen was struggling and squawking in his arms!

Tadhg nearly fainted with fright. He threw the hen to the ground where some chickens were yelping shrilly, and they all went screaming off into the trees.

"It's a spell you've put on me!" cried Tadhg.

But the Salmon did not answer. Being wiser than his famous brother he had waited until Tadhg was struggling with the hen, and then had leaped right out of the net, and dived to the bottom of his pool.

Tadhg was simply furious. He had lost the Salmon, he had lost the hen, and he had even lost the penny, because when the spell had worked it had vanished from his pocket. This was no dream! But he knew that if he went home empty-handed and told his story, his wife Molly would never believe him. But if the spell had worked once why not twice, or a dozen times? Tadhg searched all his pockets and found a halfpenny. He turned it over three times and shoved it back.

"Gnuph—knug—grumch—phunsthse," said a deep voice at his feet, and there was a fat pig with several fat piglets.

"Boys-a-boys," cried Tadhg, hugging himself with delight. "This is better than poaching any day," and he drove the pig and her young ones home to his little cottage in the heart of the woods.

"Where in the world did you steal those from?" gasped Molly when she saw the pigs.

Tadhg told her all about it but she refused to believe him.

"It's true," he protested. "I can change any Irish coin into the animal that's on it."

Molly took a jug down from the top of the dresser and fished a threepenny piece out of it. "All right," she said. "Try out your fairy tale on that, but mind you give me my threepence back."

Tadhg turned the coin three times and slipped it into his pocket. Next second a hare started up from behind the pile of wood by the hearth, bounded over Molly's feet, and out through the open door.

"Oh!" screamed Molly. "Where did that come from. It put the heart across me so it did. Do you mean to say that was the hare on the threepenny bit? Then it's true! Tadhg, we're made up, so we are. I'll sell that pig, and get a pile of pennies and start a poultry farm, so I will!"

"We'll get a half crown and have a horse," shouted Tadhg. "Our fortunes are made! Boys-a-boys, that was a great catch, that Salmon!"

Before very long word got about the district that Tadhg and Molly must have come in for a lot of money. Molly sold a fine sow and litter, and bought a new dress, an apron, and large quantities of poultry feed. Then Tadhg went to the next horse fair with a team of four splendid horses. He went home with his pockets full of money, all in small change, and a cart-load of kitchen furniture and china. He needed these because he had been foolish enough to change a shilling into a bull one evening in the kitchen. It had wrecked all the furniture and broken all the china before they had succeeded in driving it out into the woods, where it roamed about on its own and terrified everybody.

At last all this talk, of how rich Tadhg the Poacher and his wife had become reached the ears of the Sergeant, and he decided to look into the matter. He knew Tadhg was a poacher, but he had never been able to prove it. He could not see how they had come by horses and pigs, just from poaching the river, but he was sure there was something odd behind it all.

So off he went, one day, through the woods. Fortunately he wasn't far from the cottage when he heard a terrible roar behind him. He swung round, and there was the bull charging straight at him. The Sergeant had never run so fast in his life as he ran that day. He sprinted for the cottage, with the bull bellowing behind him, and just managed to reach it in time. He dashed into the kitchen and slammed the door, just as the bull hit with a dreadful crash against it. "Do you own that bull?" yelled the Sergeant.

"Yes," said Tadhg. "I mean, no! Of course not. I don't know anything about him. Won't you sit down, Sergeant, and rest? What can I do for you?"

"I want you to answer a few questions," said the Sergeant grimly. "You and your wife are mighty rich all of a sudden. Where did it all come from? And, by jingo, where did those salmon come from? Answer me that, now?" And he pointed accusingly to three beautiful salmon which lay on the kitchen table.

Now seeing that they could get a hen for a penny, Molly and Tadhg had been eating roast chicken every day for breakfast, dinner, and supper. On that very day Tadhg had declared that he couldn't touch another mouthful. Molly herself was hankering after the old poaching days, so she gave Tadhg three two-shilling pieces, and he turned them into three beautiful salmon for her. She had been ready to start cleaning them when the Sergeant had burst in.

"This is the proof I've always needed," said the Sergeant, highly delighted with himself. "You're in a bit of trouble now, Tadhg my boy. And by the way, have you a license for that big dog?"

"Sure why would I be paying a license for him when he only cost me sixpence?" cried Tadhg desperately. "Listen, Sergeant, and I'll explain everything."

He told the Sergeant that he had got the dog off a sixpence. He told him all about the spell that the Salmon had laid on him. But the Sergeant simply roared with laughter, picked up a sack that he found in the corner, and put the three salmon into it.

"I'm taking these," he said.

"Just give me a two-shilling piece, and I'll show you that it's true, what I'm telling you," begged Tadhg.

"I'll give you nothing of the sort," snapped the

Sergeant. "But I'll trouble you to come down to the barracks with me!"

"Here's a penny, Tadhg. Make it into a hen then," cried Molly. "Show him that we're speaking the truth, strange as it sounds. And sure the Sergeant can have the hen for himself, and take it home and have it for his dinner tomorrow."

Tadhg took the penny, turned it three times and put it in his pocket and—nothing happened. He tried the spell again, and still no hen appeared. The Wise Salmon had been right—the spell would only last for a short time. The Sergeant laughed loudly.

"That's a good story," he cried.

Just then the most dreadful row broke out. They all dashed to the window and saw a shocking sight. The bull had smashed the hen house to pieces and the hens were flying squawking into the woods. One minute there were a fine lot of hens there—next minute there was not a feather of them to be seen.

"Oooh, oooh!" wailed Molly. "My fine hens! Oooh!"

And at that the huge dog gave a roar of anger, sprang out of the window, and dashed at the bull. They both rushed off into the trees, barking and bellowing. In fact, nothing was left, from all that the spell had made, except the three salmon in the Sergeant's sack.

And, of course, that was the way that the brother of the famous Salmon of Knowledge intended that it should be. He was so wise that he knew all about it, and he was lying in his deep pool in the river at that very minute enjoying it all. Salmon cannot laugh, but he was getting as near to it as a fish possibly can.

Tadhg was arrested for poaching, and as he couldn't pay a fine he was sent to jail for a month. As soon as he was free he got out his nets and hurried to the river but—not a fish did he catch. He tried and tried, night after night, and at last he decided that the salmon had completely deserted the river. In the end he was forced to give up trying to poach, and had to work for his living.

There are still no salmon in that river, or so it seems. Not a fin of a salmon ever flips through the water and that, of course, is because the brother of the Salmon of Knowledge has forbidden them to come there, for fear Tadhg starts poaching again. But the Wise Salmon is there himself, lying deep in his pool, so heavy with his great knowledge that he does not ever want to come to the surface of the water.

THE

THREE BROTHERS

AND THE

TREACLE TOFFEE

——————— ✾ ✾ ✾ ———————

THE three old brothers were not of the race of the little cobbler-leprechauns, but something much superior. They were makers of new shoes, and in their little stone house, under the thorn tree of Ballylupra, footwear was made for all the fairy folk of Ireland.

Green Cap, the eldest, cut out the shoes; Red Cap stitched the uppers; and Brown Cap hammered on the soles and heels. For over three hundred years they had divided the work like this, toiling away, and only snatching a few hours of sleep at midday— which was their bedtime.

But one day Red Cap suddenly put down his needle and his waxed thread.

"I'm going to take a holiday," he said.

"Take a *what?*" said Green Cap.

"A holiday," said Red Cap. "Why not?"

Brown Cap took a handful of nails out of his mouth. "If you're tired we could have supper, and work later afterwards," he suggested.

"I don't mean that," snapped Red Cap. "I said *holiday*. I've worked for three hundred years without going on holiday, and no other worker in Ireland does that."

"But we don't go on holidays," protested Brown Cap. "And we've too much work to do."

"Where were you thinking of going—if I might ask you, Brother?" said Green Cap.

"I'm going to Wales," said Red Cap. "And you needn't argue, for my mind's made up. Isn't it the talk of Ballylupra that some of the men are going over to the big football match? Well, I'm going with them, and I'm going to hide myself in Mike Hurley's great big suitcase. I saw it out airing this morning when I was collecting the milk. I've thought the whole thing out."

"I don't know what's come over him," said Brown Cap, stroking his long beard thoughtfully. "Maybe he's not well. Do you remember how he sneezed twice last Christmas?"

"Aye, that's so," said Green Cap. "And he started sighing at his work about twenty years ago. Maybe he does need a holiday after all. Queer how we never thought of such things before. Well, we must just work harder while he's away."

But when Red Cap had gone hurrying off to hide in Mike Hurley's suitcase, Brown Cap threw down his hammer in dismay.

"We can't go on without him," he said.

"Why not?" said his brother. "We don't want holidays."

"No, and *you* could go on cutting out," agreed Brown Cap. "But I can't hammer heels and soles on shoes that haven't been stitched together; so it seems we must take a holiday, too."

"We could whitewash the kitchen then," said Green Cap. "And tidy up the place a bit. It needs it."

Well, as the brothers hadn't stopped shoemaking for three hundred years the kitchen certainly *did* need to be cleaned. The two stay-at-homes had a busy few days, and were tired and cross when Red Cap eventually came home, looking very pleased with himself.

"Have a nice time?" asked Green Cap sourly.

"It was a bit bumpy coming back," admitted Red Cap. "Mike had his case full of tins of Welsh Treacle Toffee for the children. But apart from that I've had a splendid time. But I must say, Brothers, you've made the place look quite different. It will be grand for the wedding."

"Wedding?" said Green Cap.

"What's that? Whose w-w-wedding?" stammered Brown Cap.

"Mine," said Red Cap. "I've decided that we've been bachelors too long, with nobody to cook or clean for us."

And while the other two stared at him, simply speechless, he opened his pack and took out a little Welsh lady doll, with a black skirt, check apron, red cloak, and tall black hat.

"Listen, now," he said. "Listen, Brothers. There are hundreds of these dolls in the shops, just as they have leprechaun dolls in Irish shops. I didn't actually see any ladies like this, but of course, I was with Mike and the lads, and couldn't get away to the fields to look for one. But I've decided to go back and choose a wife for myself at my leisure."

"You will not so!" cried Green Cap. "Our people don't marry. And anyway, you're much too old to get such foolish ideas."

They argued so much about it, and so loudly, that the Gray Banshee, who was blowing past in a swirl of mist, popped into the kitchen to see what the row was about.

"Ah, now, you must have some sense, Red Cap," she shrilled, when she had heard the story. "Nobody in Wales dresses like that now, except a few old witches. You couldn't ask your brothers to take a horrible old witch into the family, now could you?"

"I'm sure there must be nice ones, too," said Red Cap, looking wistfully at the doll. "But of course, if everyone is against me I won't say anymore—"

Well, he didn't say anymore, but he sighed so much at his work that Green Cap got a cold in the head from the draught, and Brown Cap's nails were blown from his bench about six times a day.

"What are we to do?" Green Cap asked his brother wildly. "He's sick, so he is."

"That's so," said Brown Cap. "He's getting thin, and he won't drink his milk—just sighs and says he wishes he had some treacle toffee—and then gazes at that doll of his."

"Something must be done," said Green Cap. "Maybe the Gray Banshee could help us? She's very wise."

So the two of them slipped away one evening and visited the Gray Banshee.

"We're thinking that poor Red Cap will fade away and die if we don't get him one of those witches you were telling us about," Brown Cap told her.

"He might die—or again he mightn't," said the

Banshee. "But you'll lose your customers, sure as eggs are eggs! I've heard that the boots that you're making now squeak, and who ever heard of fairy folk in squeaking boots? Silly little men that you are!"

But after a lot of talk, and when they had given her a golden necklace, the Banshee agreed to go over to Wales and seek out the nicest, gentlest witch and bring her back to Red Cap, to be his bride. So the Banshee wrapped herself in a cloud and off she went but—alas that the leprechauns could not guess—she had no intention of carrying out her part of the bargain. She was really furious. Leprechauns didn't marry. But if they did, why couldn't Red Cap choose an Irish wife? What about her, for instance, the handsomest Banshee in the country?

Now at that very minute, in the depths of a Welsh forest, Tall Hat the witch was stirring a sticky black brew in a big black pot, quite unaware that the Banshee had started her journey with a heart full of ill-will. But Tall Hat had just heard another bit of news, for her black cat had come dashing up to tell her that there was to be a big witches' conference that very night, and that Tall Hat must attend.

"Oh, dear, dear!" wailed Tall Hat, and dropped her ladle right into the pot.

The reason for her dismay was that Tall Hat was *not* a successful witch. She had no talent for wickedness, and she didn't even look the part. Her cheeks stayed rosy, even though she rubbed flour on her face, and she hated the all-black witches' uniform so much that in secret she had made check aprons and a red cloak for herself.

And now she simply dare not refuse to go to the conference, although she had no wicked deeds to report, and had made no poison brews in her pot for years—nothing but toffee, of which she and the cat were very fond.

"Oh, dear," wailed Tall Hat. "I'll be punished for this!" But she collected her cat and broomstick and set off.

The witches met at midnight in a churchyard, and each in turn had to recount her activities, and very horrible they were! Tall Hat was simply shaking with fear and, as a matter of fact, so was the Gray Banshee, who happened to be hiding in the belfry in company with the bats.

"What an insult that Red Cap should want one of these creatures," she said angrily to herself. "Serves him right if I pick out the very nastiest of them, and offer her my gold necklace if she'll come to Ireland and marry Red Cap! Yes, that's just what I'll do!"

And the Gray Banshee crept softly down the stairs of the belfry, just as Tall Hat's black cat began to creep softly up to see if she could catch some bats.

What a shock they both got, but the Banshee was the first to recover.

"Tell me now, Pussy," she whispered. "Which is the wickedest witch here?"

"Oh, that one in the red cloak," said the faithful cat promptly. "She's simply awful!"

"Not married?" asked the Banshee eagerly.

"Who'd marry that nasty creature?" said the cat.

At that the Banshee let out a screech of laughter—

"Oooooooooooh!" she went, and the witches, who had never heard a Banshee in full howl before, were simply terrified. They jumped on their broomsticks and—whiz—off they went. All except Tall Hat who was never very good at broomstick riding, and was too terrified to make a proper takeoff.

But the Banshee mistook this for courage. "I'm only a poor Irish Banshee, your Wickedness," she said. "Listen, now, and I'll tell you how a clever witch like yourself can make a pile of money."

Tall Hat was too frightened to speak, but she made horrible faces. Then the Banshee told her all about Red Cap, and how he was falling ill because he wanted a little wife from Wales. Tall Hat, whose heart was very soft, nearly said, "Ah, the poor creature!" but she choked it back in time, and it sounded like a very evil spell instead.

"Will you come?" begged the Banshee, throwing the gold necklace round Tall Hat's neck. "The three brothers have a whole sack of gold besides this."

Tall Hat would have gone to the North Pole at that very minute to escape from the other witches, so she nodded her head, and before she had time to worry about mounting her broomstick, the Banshee had caught her up in a gray cloud and carried her off. And the poor cat jumped on the broomstick and followed as fast as she could.

Well, in Ballylupra every fairy for miles around had gathered to see Red Cap's bride arriving, and when they saw Tall Hat, who was still making horrible faces, they looked at one another in dismay. But the wedding took place, with much feasting, and then the guests all went away, and the Banshee went off and laughed so much that she lost her voice and couldn't scream for a week.

As soon as she felt better she went to visit the brothers. She had decided that if they were *very* miserable she might relent, and weave a counter-spell to make Tall Hat powerless.

Outside the stone house she found the cat basking in the sun, and a lineful of check aprons hanging out to dry. And inside—well, inside the three brothers were working, faster than ever before, and they were all munching away like mad. Tall Hat, with her

cheeks flushed, was cutting up a fresh tray of toffee, and all were looking so happy that the Banshee's anger flared up again.

She opened her mouth to scream but at that moment Tall Hat popped a big bit of treacle toffee into it, and she could only say—"Um-mum-um," instead.

It was simply delicious toffee, but it was also magical. As it melted, the Banshee's resentment melted, too. By the time her jaws were free she merely wanted to tell Tall Hat how glad she was that everything had turned out so well, and to welcome her to Ballylupra.

And indeed, so strong was the magic that Tall Hat and the Banshee remained the very best of neighbors. The three brothers gave another golden necklace to the Banshee, who came to visit them almost every evening, to chat with Tall Hat and eat treacle toffee. It is said that Ballylupra has the sweetest voiced Banshee in all Ireland!

CHRISTIE

AND THE

GROWING HAND

———— ✿ ✿ ✿ ————

CHRISTIE and Martin Duffy were two old brothers who ran a nursery garden and spent their lives working in it. But there was not a great deal of happiness in the garden, because Christie was bitterly jealous of his brother. The reason for this was that everything that Martin planted grew so well that nobody ever looked twice at Christie's flowers and vegetables.

"Don't I work just as hard as you, Brother?" Christie would complain. "Isn't it the same soil, and doesn't the same rain fall on it, and the same sun shine on it?"

"To be sure," Martin would say. "But then you haven't got the knack with flowers. You haven't got the growing hand, and that makes all the difference."

"Stuff and nonsense!" Christie would snort, and he would work with more care than ever. Well—his plants were very nice, there was no denying it, but although Martin took less trouble, and spent a lot of his time leaning over the garden gate and smoking his pipe, his flowers were always far more beautiful than his brother's. And as for his vegetables—people came miles to buy them, and never took the trouble to ask the price of those that Christie had grown.

Well, Christie kept brooding about the whole matter, and before long he was as thin as a runner bean and his face was as gray as his whiskers. One day the old Herb Woman paid them a visit, and her eyes nearly popped out of her head when she saw the change in Christie.

"What ails you at all, man?" she said. "If it's ill you are you should tell me about it, and maybe I've got a potion or an ointment that would help you."

Christie led the old woman into a quiet corner of the garden where Martin could not hear them.

"Tell me, ma'am," he said, pointing to a turnip, "what might that be?"

The Herb Woman looked at the turnip and her eyes lit up.

"That is a very fine turnip," she said. "If it's giving it to me you are, then thank you kindly!"

"I'm not giving it to you," snapped Christie. "It

was my brother that grew it. But tell me, what is that?"

The Herb Woman was getting annoyed. "That's a miserable little runt of a cabbage," she snapped. "Do you think I'm blind?"

"I grew that cabbage—" began Christie.

"Shame on you for a nursery gardener!" interrupted the Herb Woman. "There's no doubt about it—*you* haven't the growing hand!"

"That's just it," cried Christie excitedly. "It's an awful thing for me not to have it, living with Martin, too. It has me worried to death. Can you brew me a potion that will give me a better way with the plants?"

Now the Herb Woman was known all over the country for the cures that she had worked. Not only did people shake off colds and fevers when she attended them, it was said that lameness, baldness, and even bad temper had been cured by her potions. People said that when she wandered through the fields in the evenings, picking herbs and grasses, she had picked up a good bit of magic from the fairy folk.

"Well—" said the Herb Woman. "We could try. If I make a potion for you will you give me the full of my arms of your brother's vegetables?"

Of course, Christie should have refused but—

"Sure when I get the growing hand I'll pay him back, and more than pay him," he said to himself, and he told the Herb Woman to make the brew, and to make it as strong as possible.

For the next few days Christie was simply on edge with excitement, and at last, one evening, the Herb Woman came back and gave him a black bottle, full of thick stuff, that smelled very nasty indeed!

"Drink it all down," she commanded, "and while you're busy I'll just go down the garden and gather the few bits of vegetables for myself."

Martin was in the kitchen, dozing, so Christie nodded to the Herb Woman and began to drink the mixture. Well—it had looked bad, and it had smelled worse, but that was nothing to the taste. Christie felt that it would kill him to drink it, but he wanted so much to have the growing hand that he forced himself to swallow it all. While he was struggling with the potion the Herb Woman was very busy, and when she staggered off with her payment Christie told himself that he had never seen one old woman carry so much!

Anyway, he soon forgot to worry about Martin's vegetables; he seized his hoe and went out to work with his own.

"I wonder how long it will take to work?" he said to himself after hoeing one of his flower beds. He leaned on the hoe to rest, for he was still feeling rather ill after the Herb Woman's potion. And just then Martin came into the garden.

"Aye, Brother, that's a wonderful sunflower!" exclaimed Martin.

"Where!" said Christie, looking along the flower bed. "The one you're holding," said Martin. "Careful, or you'll break the stem."

Christie was going to answer that he wasn't holding any sunflower, when he looked above him, and saw a huge yellow flower just over his head. Then he looked at the handle of the hoe, and found that it was the sunflower's stem.

"I—I—I'm not feeling very well," he said. "I'm imagining things. I'm going in to sit in the kitchen and rest."

He let go of the sunflower, went into the kitchen, and shut the door after him.

"I was sure I had a hoe in my hand," he said to himself, pulling forward a chair and sinking into it.

He was still sitting there, with his eyes shut, when Martin came hurrying in. He had just discovered how many of his beautiful vegetables were missing.

"Brother," he exclaimed, "I've been robbed and, what's more, somebody has played a horrible joke on

us. He's taken away the door and put a trellis of roses in its place. We must call the police!"

"Don't be silly," snapped Christie. "I closed the door myself a minute ago and—" Just then he opened his eyes and they almost fell out of his head with surprise. Martin was right, and a basket-work trellis of the most beautiful roses hung from the doorpost!

Christie gripped the arms of his chair. "I'm ill," he faltered, and then felt the chair arms snapping like twigs under his hands. He was afraid to look—and yet he had to look. He was sitting in a chair neatly cut from a bush of privet!

"Brother," he screamed, clutching the table. "I'm bewitched!"

Under his hand the table had put roots through the floor, and turned into a sawed-off, but living, tree stump. Martin watched, swallowed, and said weakly. "So I see, Brother. But might I ask—how?"

Red with shame, Christie told him all about the Herb Woman and her potion.

"Maybe it will wear off," said Martin. "And again —maybe it won't. Brother, be careful, you must not touch anything more!"

Christie had just taken his pipe from the dresser, and it had turned into a carrot in his hand. "But how am I to live?" he cried. "I've got to eat and dress."

"I heard a story of a king once," said Martin. "Everything that he touched turned into gold, and in the end he died. You won't starve, Brother, but you'll get a bit tired of raw vegetables."

"I'll use a knife and fork," cried Christie, who loved a well-cooked dinner. He seized a knife from the dresser and it turned into a willow branch.

"Stop destroying our things," cried Martin. "Keep your hands in the air! When you're hungry I'll feed you with a spoon. But the most important thing is to find that Herb Woman."

But the brothers found that the Herb Woman was not easy to find. She was enjoying Martin's vegetables so much that she wanted to keep out of his way. Day after day poor Christie sat at home, trying to remember not to touch anything, while Martin scoured the country searching for the old woman. And at last he found her.

"You're welcome to what my brother gave you," he said, "and you can have as many more if you can take the growing hand away from him again."

"I'm not at all sure about that," wailed the Herb Woman. "That was the strongest brew I've ever made. I'll give you a box of ointment for his hands, but I'm not promising that it will be strong enough to fight the potion."

"We must try it anyway," said Martin. "And thank

you, ma'am. You're not to blame for the foolish jealousy that forced my brother to turn to magic."

Martin carried the box of ointment carefully home and poor Christie seized it and rubbed it on his hands, then he touched a cup and it immediately turned into a large rose.

"That's not much good," said Martin, and then they both stared in horror at Christie's hands. The ointment itself was affected by the power of growing, and Christie's hands were covered with soft green moss, that refused to come off no matter how he scraped at them with his nails.

After that Christie never left the house, except at night when he used to wander sadly through the fields. And one night as he walked he heard a sorrowful little voice wailing, accompanied by a tap-tap-tapping, and came upon a little green man tapping away at a shoe and sighing to himself.

"What's wrong?" asked Christie. "You seem as old and as sad as I am myself."

"Och, mo bhron," said the little man. "My lovely thorn tree is killed on me. I've no home any more." And he kept tapping at his shoe.

"Who in this district would harm a thorn tree?" asked Christie. "Can't you get your own back on him? I thought you people could look after yourselves. Will you stop that tapping! My nerves are bad."

"A flash of lightning hasn't any cows that I can drive astray, or a churn that I can upset," snapped the little man, and went on tapping.

At that Christie forgot himself, and grasped the little man's hammer from his hand. It turned into a bunch of radishes, and the little man's mouth fell open with surprise.

"So you're under a spell," he exclaimed. "That's why you came upon me so suddenly, and I didn't hear you. I was wondering if you had something magical about you. Well, well, so you've had an overdose of the growing hand! That Herb Woman will go to jail some one of these days—but if you human beings are so silly—!"

"Listen," pleaded Christie. "I know I was a poor, silly old man, but is there anything that can be done for me?"

"There might—" admitted the little green man. "I'm thinkin', Christie Duffy, if you were to touch my thorn tree it would grow again. And then I'll promise to get your hands clean for you."

Christie was delighted to agree and they hurried off to the field where the poor thorn tree had been killed by the lightning; Christie touched the tree with the growing hands and the tree put out leaves, and even burst into flower, although it was long past blossom time.

"Now, rub your hands in the dew under the tree,"

cried the little green man. "Good-bye, and good luck," and he dived into a hole in the tree.

Well, it was as he had said. Christie went home without the growing hand, and shook Martin awake to tell him the news. At first Martin was terrified, thinking that *he* would turn into something growing. But then—"Well, Brother," he said, "I don't suppose there'll be any more jealousy or trouble to make us unhappy with one another."

Nor was there—Christie was only too glad to let Martin do the planting while he tackled the weeding.

MALACHI AND

RED CAP

THE LEPRECHAUN

❀ ❀ ❀

THERE was not a doubt in the world that Malachi
was the meanest old man in Ireland. Even his sister
Minnie, who lived with him, had to admit that he
was such a miser that he would have tried to crawl
down a mousehole to find a lost halfpenny. Indeed
there was a joke made in the district about poor
Malachi's bald head. The people used to say that he
must have sold his hair to the Little People to fill
their pillows with.

Malachi didn't care what was said about him. As
long as he got a good price for his milk and his eggs,
his potatoes and his wheat, that was all that mat-
tered—provided Minnie didn't get hold of too much

of the money, and waste it on things they didn't need. Even the beggar folk knew that it was no good to call at Malachi's farm, because poor Minnie was afraid to give them as much as a cup of tea.

And then one evening Malachi discovered that *somebody* was helping himself to fresh milk, taking it out of the big can in the dairy, and that although Minnie had suspected this for a long time she had said nothing. Malachi was simply furious!

"I'll catch the thief if I have to hide in the dairy all day and all night," he stormed.

"Ah, sure it's only about a cupful that's missing," said Minnie. "It might well be that some of the Little People from the old thorn tree had need of a drop of sweet milk!"

"Little People or not," shouted Malachi, "it's my milk. Nobody's going to take milk from under my nose without paying for it!"

So Malachi hid behind the churn in the dairy, and that was how he trapped Red Cap the Leprechaun when the little fellow came as usual with his wooden bowl to get the milk for his supper. Malachi waited until Red Cap was busy at the can, and then he sprang out from behind the churn and stood in the doorway, simply spluttering with rage.

"Caught you in the act," he said. "Well, what have you to say for yourself?"

Poor Red Cap had got such a surprise that he had spilled some of the milk down the front of his green tunic. He put his bowl carefully down and looked into Malachi's furious face.

"And what have you to say for yourself, you old miser?" he asked calmly. "You grudge me the few feet of soil in the field where my thorn tree grows. You've cut so close to it with your plough that you've destroyed the roots on me, and the tree's getting crookeder with every big wind. What have you to say for yourself?"

Malachi nearly choked with rage. It was true that he hated to have the old thorn tree in his field. He would have cut it down only he was afraid of ill-luck. But here was the little creature of a leprechaun, caught red-handed stealing milk, and he hadn't even the grace to apologize. He wasn't a young fellow either, whom one could perhaps excuse. His ugly little face looked hundreds of years old, and his long beard was snow white.

"You ought to be ashamed of yourself," spluttered Malachi. "I could have cut your tree down years ago, and had a nice armful of corn from the ground where it grows. And all the thanks I get is to have the milk stolen from the can."

"Stolen!" exclaimed Red Cap. "Haven't I had milk from your father, and his father before him? And your grandmother used to make the sweetest bit of cheese I've ever tasted, and always a bit left on the windowsill for Red Cap the Leprechaun! And now in my old age you expect to be paid for what I take! How should I pay you?"

Malachi said nothing, but he thought one word, and it echoed deep down inside his mind. "Gold!" thought Malachi. He began to plan how he could force Red Cap to lead him to his crock of gold if only he could keep his eyes on the little fellow, because everybody knows that a leprechaun is helpless as long as one keeps watching him. Yes, Red Cap must pay him in gold, not only for the milk that he had got from him all these years, but for what he had taken from Malachi's father and grandfather as well. It would take a nice crock of gold for all that!

Suddenly, without warning, Malachi made a grab for the leprechaun, but Red Cap twisted sideways and threw his red cap into Malachi's face. For a split second Malachi could not see him, and in that split second the leprechaun skipped behind the milk can.

Now when the red cap hit Malachi it did a very strange thing. It struck his face, but then it climbed up his forehead and back to his bald head, and there it settled itself down, and when Malachi grasped it not an inch would it move, no matter how he tugged.

"So you would take my gold?" said Red Cap's voice from behind the milk can, and when Malachi moved round the can the voice moved, too, so that the can was still between them. "So you would grow corn on the few feet of soil where my tree grows? So you grudge me the sup of milk to wet my lips, do you? I'll give you corn—and here's for your milk—" and with that Red Cap tipped over the can, so that the milk flowed over Malachi's feet. And while the old miser danced with rage the leprechaun was out of the door in a flash and gone.

Minnie heard the clatter of the can, and came dashing in to find her brother dancing about in a pool of milk with a red cap on his head.

"What's wrong with you at all?" she cried. "Take that silly thing off your head."

But that Malachi could not do. He told his sister how the leprechaun had got the better of him, and Minnie was not in the least sorry for him.

"You're bewitched, you silly old man, and it's what you deserve," she declared, and she caught hold of the red cap and pulled with all her strength.

"Ow, ow! You'll take the ears off me," shrieked Malachi.

Minnie stopped pulling and put her head on one side because she could think better that way. "Brother," she said, "take some of the fresh eggs out of the basket, and off with you up to the thorn tree. Apologize to that leprechaun for being so rude to him, and give him the eggs to make it up with him."

"Me! Apologize to *him!*" shouted Malachi. "Not if I have to wear his red cap for the rest of my life!"

"All right, just wait until the neighbors see it," said Minnie.

But Malachi did not like that idea either. As the days went past he was careful not to be seen. But the trouble with that was that he had to let Minnie bargain with the Egg Buyer when he came round, and he had a feeling that Minnie did not give him all the money, but slipped some of it into her apron pocket. And then when they needed groceries and oil from the village he had to let his sister go to do the shopping. Minnie was delighted. She bought a lot of things that Malachi considered mere luxuries and waste of money, and she brought him back no change at all.

"I'll be ruined," wailed Malachi, and tugged at the red cap. "I don't see how it can cling so fast," he complained. "My head is as smooth as an egg." He felt his head through the cap, and his face suddenly lit up. "Minnie," he gasped. "It's a magic cap all right. I think I'm growing hair under it! Feel!"

Minnie felt his head through the red cap. "Sure enough, there's something growing," she said. "But what's the use of growing hair when nobody can see it with that thing on your head?"

"It's growing very fast and strong," said Malachi. "When it gets long enough it will push the red cap off. I wonder what color it will be?"

"White or gray," said Minnie. "You're too old for anything else."

"Maybe not," said Malachi. "It's a magic cap, isn't it?"

"Well, you're a vain old fool, sure enough," exclaimed Minnie. But they were both very curious about Malachi's hair all the same. The next time the Egg Buyer came round Malachi greeted him, red cap and all, and drove an even harder bargain than usual.

"This is a special new hair restorer," he explained airily. "I'll have a fine head of hair by next week."

And indeed, that seemed likely, for the pressure inside the cap was so great that it was standing straight up, and one of the seams began to gape with the strain. At this Minnie could contain herself no longer. She widened the split with her scissors and peered inside.

"Oh, oh! Murder! We're ruined altogether!" she screamed. "It's green hair you've grown, Brother! Oh, oh!"

Malachi reached up in alarm, and poked a finger

through the split in the cap. It certainly did not feel like hair.

"Look again. Feel it!" he begged Minnie in a trembling voice.

Minnie pulled some of the stuff through the split and screamed again. "Oh, oh, it's not hair!" she cried. "You're growing corn on the top of your head, so you are!"

Now Malachi understood how well the leprechaun was punishing him. So that was what he had meant when he had abused Malachi for wanting to grow corn where the tree stood. "I'll give you corn!" he had said. And this was where he had grown it.

It was too much. Malachi knew when he was beaten. That night when dusk was falling he made his way to the thorn tree. He had two dozen eggs in a basket and a pound of fresh butter.

"Red Cap," he called gently, and tapped on the trunk of the tree.

Red Cap was awake and listening, but he gave a great snore, and winked to himself.

"Red Cap," pleaded Malachi, louder this time. "Please listen to me. I've got a few eggs and some butter for you, and you can come for milk any evening you like."

"Go away," came Red Cap's voice from the center of the tree. "I want to go to sleep."

"No, no," wailed Malachi. "Please take this dreadful stuff off my head!"

"It's very fine corn," answered Red Cap. "You should keep it and sell it."

"I don't want to sell corn from my head," wailed Malachi. "I'll get Minnie to make soda bread for you, so I will. And I'll put a support at your tree so that the wind won't hurt it."

Red Cap considered. He was getting lonely without his cap. He could not sleep without it because his ears got cold. And anyway he had had his fun. "Will you put a fence round my tree?" he asked. "A nice wooden fence with a little gate in it."

"I will surely," said Malachi eagerly. "I'll do anything you ask."

"All right," said Red Cap, and Malachi felt the cap plucked from his head. Anxiously he felt his scalp. It was as bald as an egg.

How pleased he was! He danced round the thorn tree and called Red Cap the nicest, kindest, and most gentlemanly leprechaun he had ever met. But Red Cap snored again, and this time he was really asleep. He had pulled his dear red cap over his ears and gone off to sleep at once. So Malachi put down the eggs and butter and went dancing home to Minnie. He kept his promise to Red Cap, nor was he mean to anybody else again. He had only to run his hand over his bald head to remember what had been there—and when he thought of the red cap and the corn, he shuddered, and gave freely to anybody who asked for help.

THE BANSHEE'S

BIRTHDAY TREAT

————— ❀ ❀ ❀ —————

SAMMY the Shoemaker lived all alone, a good two miles from the town of Ballycrockshee. Some people said he lived far from the town in order that customers would wear out another pair of shoes, going to collect the mended ones from Sammy. And others said that the old man had friends and customers amongst the fairy people of the hills, and that they had heard voices and laughter in his cottage when they approached it and then found Sammy alone after all.

Well, Sammy *had* some rather odd friends, and so he wasn't alarmed when there was a loud thumping on his door late one night. He wasn't alarmed, but he *was* annoyed, for he had locked his doors, eaten his supper, put out his lamp, and was warming the big cozy nightcap in which he always slept.

Bang bang—rattle rattle! went the door. And then a shrill woman's voice called his name.

Sammy jammed the nightcap on his round head, and opened the door. "Well?" he demanded, when a very tall, very thin, very gray old woman had slipped into the kitchen. "Didn't the boots fit you? You've only had them twelve hours, and you must give them time to wear in."

"Wear in!" The old woman cackled with laughter. "Wear out, you mean! Look at them!"

She held out a foot, on which the battered remains of a gray boot was hanging. "I need them mended by morning, Sammy," she ordered.

At first Sammy was speechless. He gazed at the Gray Banshee, for that was who she was, and finally he got back his voice. "What have you been doing with them?" he spluttered. "The nicest, softest boots I've ever made, and in a few hours you have them in shreds!"

"I was at a bit of a dance at the Fort," admitted the Banshee. "I was doing a set with the Pooka, and he tramped the boots off me with his clumsy big hooves, to say nothing of the state of my corns!"

"Serves you right," snapped Sammy. "Dancing at your age, and with the fairy horse, too!"

"Age!" The Banshee drew herself up until she was almost twice as tall as the little man. "I'm only five hundred years old tomorrow. That's nothing for a Banshee. And I'm going to give myself a birthday treat and go down to the Fun Fair at Ten-Mile-Town, and that's why I must have the boots mended by the morning. I've heard that there are wonderful Hobbyhorses at the Fair and I told the Pooka I was going, just to make him jealous. He thinks there's no horse to equal him in Ireland, and I've heard that Hobbyhorses go dancing round to music. I'm sure they don't destroy a decent woman's new boots!" And she shook the boots angrily from her feet.

"Now, listen," said Sammy firmly. "I was just going to go to bed. I'm sorry about your birthday but—"

He stopped short, because a change had come over the Banshee. She began to shake, and to draw long breaths and let them out with violent puffs. In fact—the Banshee was going to screech. Some Banshees screech at will, but Sammy knew that with his friend screeching was like sneezing. She just couldn't stop herself.

"All right!" yelled Sammy. "I'll have the boots ready. Don't let go until you get outside!" He pushed the Banshee through the door and slammed it, just as the most horrible wail arose from her. Then he pulled the nightcap down over his ears, and dived under his bed until the screeching had died away into the hills.

Next morning, as Sammy was finishing breakfast, the Banshee arrived barefoot and eagerly seized the boots that were waiting for her.

"Beautiful they are, and no mistake," she cried.

"Many happy returns of your birthday," said good-natured Sammy. "I hope you enjoy the Fair."

"You must come with me," cried the Banshee at once. "We'll celebrate my birthday together."

"Well," began Sammy, who had been up all night working on the boots, "I was thinking of a snooze—"

But the Banshee wouldn't take "no" for an answer, and eventually Sammy pinned a note to his door, saying he would be away that day, and they set off together.

Ten-Mile-Town was a long distance across the hills from Ballycrockshee, and soon poor Sammy began to get hot and tired. At this the Banshee calmly stepped in front of a turf truck that was approaching and the driver stopped with a screech of brakes.

"Will you take us to Ten-Mile-Town?" she asked. "My friend is tired, and we're going to see the Hobbyhorses."

"Certainly, missus," said the driver, who must

have thought them a very odd pair indeed. And they climbed up into the front seat of the truck.

"I'm having a birthday treat," said the Banshee chattily. "And I'm very fond of horses. Have you ever seen Hobbyhorses?"

"Many a time," said the driver. "Loved them when I was a child."

"And I'm five hundred years old and never saw one!" exclaimed the Banshee.

"Five hundred years!" Of course, the driver simply didn't believe her. "Ho, ho, ho! Ha, ha, ha! That's a good one."

And he chuckled to himself as if he would never stop, saying, "Five hundred years. That's a good answer," between chuckles. He would probably have laughed all the way to Ten-Mile-Town, had not something happened to the Banshee. Sammy noticed suddenly that she was beginning to shake and draw deep breaths.

"Don't," he whispered. "You can't scream here!"

Unfortunately, the Banshee could—and after great efforts to restrain herself *did* scream. At the first yell the driver lifted both hands from the wheel and clapped them over his ears.

Now they were at the top of a long, steep hill down into the town, and the truck simply charged down and along the main street with the Banshee screaming and the driver fighting to get control of his wheel again. They finished up at the end of the street in the window of a china shop, and there the Banshee's wail died away, for all the world like a mill horn.

And that was what all the girls in the nearby linen mill thought it was. They thought it was the horn to knock off work, and out they trooped into the street, over a hundred of them, laughing and shouting. This was fortunate for Sammy and the Banshee, for with such a crowd around the smashed shop window they were able to slip away before the dazed driver could stop them.

The Fun Fair did good trade that afternoon, for many of the mill girls celebrated their unusual break by going along to the Fair. Sammy had to pay the entrance money for both the Banshee and himself, for she had nothing but fairy money.

"Try a lovely strawberry ice," cried an ice-cream boy.

"Thank you kindly," said the Banshee, and then looked positively huffy when he demanded three-pence. "Sure he gave it to me!" she cried loudly.

Red to the ears, Sammy paid for the ice cream, and then when the Banshee exclaimed at the balloons bobbing on their sticks, he bought one for her. Un-fortunately, the Banshee's long, ragged nails burst the balloon and this amused her most of all. "How nicely they pop!" she cried, and she jabbed her nails into a whole row of balloons that were hanging above the stall. Poor Sammy didn't know how he should pay for all this damage, and hustled his friend away into the crowd almost before the last balloon had finished bursting.

But the Hobbyhorses were the big disappointment of the birthday for the Banshee. "Those painted, wooden things!" she cried disbelievingly. "Why they don't even go quickly, and they don't dance—just go round and round to that silly music."

"They're only a children's game," explained Sammy. "I thought you knew they weren't real horses."

"I wouldn't have come so far to see those things," said the Banshee bitterly. "But seeing that I am here I might as well ride."

And without bothering to pay, the Banshee seemed to glide through the air and landed on the back of an empty Hobbyhorse. And no sooner did it feel the Banshee on its back, than the horse began to go faster and faster, and to bounce up and down. There was a great rumpus then because all the horses began speeding round, and the music got simply left behind and got sulky and stopped altogether. Some of the children that were riding were scared and cried, but others were delighted and cheered the Banshee.

Sammy was horrified. And then he saw a group of very angry people approaching. There was the owner of the china shop, walking with the truck driver and a policeman. There was the boy from the balloon stall. There was a red-faced man, who kept shouting to groups of linen-mill girls to go back to work as somebody had played a joke and set off the horn too soon. And the truck driver kept shouting that he had been attacked at the wheel of his lorry by a tall, thin old woman and a fat, bald old man! "And there's the woman now, on the Hobbyhorses!" yelled the man.

"Run, Banshee, run," yelled poor Sammy, and darted away into the crowd himself. Indeed, he was so scared that before he knew where he was, he was crouching under an upturned cart hiding from the crowds. Oh, dear, oh, dear, why had he left his quiet cottage and joined the Banshee on this disastrous trip? And what were they going to do to his friend when they caught her?

He need not have worried about that. They couldn't catch the Banshee. She slipped through the crowd like a puff of smoke, and the Hobbyhorses, without her magic, returned to their normal slow trot. Indeed, the Banshee could have slipped right out of the town without any trouble, had it not been for her loyalty to Sammy. She slipped under the cart beside him, and he saw that two tears were trickling down her gray face.

"Everybody is angry," she said. "Sure I meant no harm. I'm thinking I'll go back home to my own place."

Sammy wanted nothing better than to go, too, and he was beginning to plan how they could hide until closing time and then slip into the dusk, when he noticed the Banshee beginning to shake and breathe hard.

"Oh, no," he pleaded. "Banshee—don't do it here!"

The Banshee tried to smother her scream. She held her nose, and pulled her shawl over her head, but when the scream did break loose it was the worst she had ever given. It blew the cart from over them and the angry crowd came running.

But just at that moment, when Sammy thought they were lost, the Pooka arrived. There was a thunder of hooves, and the wild white horse dashed through the Fair, scattering people to left and right, and making directly for his friends. The Banshee, still giving her wail, practically lifted Sammy onto the wild horse's bare back and sprang up behind him.

And away they went, like a whirlwind. Up in the hills the Pooka slowed to a trot.

"I knew you'd find no horse at the Fair to equal me," he said proudly. "Come, Banshee, there's a special birthday dance at the Fort for you tonight. Come—you shall be my partner again—and your human friend may come, too."

But Sammy begged to be left at his cottage instead. He had had enough adventures for a long time to come. He wished the Banshee a joyful evening and went gratefully to his bed, with his nightcap pulled right over his face this time.

Next morning, on his doorstep, he found a little bag of fairy money and the Banshee's boots, which were battered to pieces again. Sammy could see that she had indeed danced with the Pooka at her birthday party.

DAVID AND
THE BIG DRUM

❀ ❀ ❀

DAVID McIVOR was the principal piccolo player in the town band, as his father had been before him, and his grandfather before that.

"A very talented lad," said Old Rooney the Bandmaster. And that should have satisfied David, because Old Rooney was very hard to please. But instead of being satisfied he was most discontented because he wanted to play the big drum instead.

Oh, if only he could play the drum! He would walk behind the band, boom, boom booming. And not only that—he would go in for drumming contests, using the light, wandlike sticks, and walking round and round the town with the big drum thundering under his blows!

"I'm thinking of buying an old drum to practice on," David said to his mother one evening. "I'm tired of the piccolo."

Well, his mother laughed, and his sister Kate laughed, and a chuckle from the direction of the heap of turf near the fire told him that the Little Brown Fellow was laughing, too. David felt himself blushing. It was bad enough that his people laughed at him, but that the invisible little magical person who always sat on the McIvors' turf should laugh, too!

"Why is it so funny?" cried David.

"*You* with a big drum!" cried his mother. "And you as small and thin as a child, for all that you're a man. Why, David, have sense."

"You'd have to get somebody to carry the drum for you," cried Kate.

Well, they argued and talked and laughed, and then David's mother became suddenly serious.

"Listen, lad," she said. "Be content! You're the sweetest piccolo player there's ever been in the town, and the Brown Fellow agrees with what I'm saying. You should see him sitting there when you're playing, David, puffing his old clay pipe and nodding his head to the rhythm. So you should be well pleased with things as they are."

David wasn't a bit pleased! It always annoyed him that his mother could see the Brown Fellow, with his

wrinkled brown face, brown leather suit, and long
white beard. His grandmother had seen the creature,
too. And even young Kate, when she went to put
sods on the fire, would say, "Sorry to disturb you,
sir," quite at her ease with the creature. So David
wasn't going to take any notice of someone who only
appeared to *women*. He said nothing more, but he
was more than ever determined to play the drum.
He'd show them what he could do!

Unfortunately you can't take up drumming without the whole neighborhood knowing what you're up
to. You can't even buy a drum secretly, to say nothing of playing it. When David went into the nearest
big town, without saying a word at home, and spent
all his savings on a drum, the thing was delivered
one day on a truck and that gave the secret away at
once. His mother made him keep it in an outhouse,
and there he spent a lot of his time trying to learn to
play.

He banged and he banged. His arms ached, and
his back ached, and his head ached, and no matter
how hard he worked, evening after evening, it still
sounded like the worst drumming he had ever heard
in his life. To make matters worse, the whole town
knew about the drum.

"I suppose you're going to win the contest, David,"
his friends would say. "But you're too shy, doing

your practice at home." And the other men that were going to compete in the drumming match would walk about the roads practicing, carrying their drums as easily as if they were made of feathers.

Poor David. If he carried the drum he couldn't hit it—and if he hit the drum he couldn't carry it! On the night before the big drumming match he threw down his sticks in despair and went into the kitchen where he sat with his piccolo and played the sweetest, saddest tunes that he had ever played.

He was all alone, for his mother and Kate had taken to going visiting in the evenings to get away from the drum, and he played for a very long time before he had to pause for a rest.

"Indeed, that was a treat," said a thin old voice from the heap of turf.

"So you're there, are you?" said David crossly.

"You know well I'm here," said the voice. "I've sat by this fireside for seventy years, and very pleasant years they have been—although it's been noisy lately, with that thing you keep in the shed. Foolish you are to want to change, when you can play the piccolo so sweetly that I'd be tempted to offer you anything you'd ask if you'd play that last air to me again."

"Done!" cried David, and put the piccolo to his lips and repeated the air he had just played.

"Lovely," said the voice of the Brown Fellow. "I enjoyed that, so I did."

"Good," said David. "Now, what about my part of the bargain. You offered me anything I wished—and I'd like to be the best drummer that ever hit a drumskin!"

The neat little pile of turf sods collapsed to the ground as if the Brown Fellow had toppled off his seat.

"Oh—oh!" came his voice from the ashes of the hearth. "What a foolish old fellow I was—and what a silly wish you've made. But I'll do it for you, even though I've cracked me best pipe on the ground!"

He hadn't finished speaking before David felt a strange tingling running down his two arms down to his fingertips. Out he dashed to the shed and began to beat the drum like mad. And this time there was no doubt about it—he really was a drummer. There wasn't a better drummer in the country and he had no more difficulty in carrying the drum, big as it was.

When Mrs. McIvor and Kate came home later on they heard the thunder of the drum in the shed, but wisely they left David by himself.

"Sure the contest is tomorrow," said Kate. "And anyway, he's really mastered the drumming at last. Peter the Blacksmith isn't able to do it better."

David banged the drum all night and hardly took time to eat the breakfast that his mother brought him. Indeed, his hands jerked and twitched all the time longing to be at the drum.

"Rest yourself, lad," pleaded his mother.

"I can't," David said, and indeed that was the truth. He simply could not stop playing the drum, even when he tried.

Well, he played all day and marched off playing to the contest that evening. The town band led the way to the field where the drumming match was to be held—and very cross they all were because David wouldn't play his piccolo as usual, but followed the band, banging and thundering on his drum so loudly that the others need not have bothered to play. Old Rooney the Bandmaster shouted himself hoarse, but David would not stop—*could* not stop.

The rules of a drumming match vary according to the district, but in all places one rule is the same. The best drummer is he who can go on longest and loudest. Well, nobody had a chance against the magic that the Brown Fellow had put in David's arms. Even Peter the Blacksmith, who always won the contest, had to give in eventually, and David drummed his way home followed by a cheering crowd.

"And now, lad," commanded his mother. "Away

with the drum and eat your supper and get some sleep!"

David was hungry and sleepy, but still. he couldn't stop his arms from beating the drum. Kate and his mother took it from him at last, and locked it in the shed, but still his arms went like a pair of flails, and swept all the china from the table when he sat down to his supper.

"It's all the Brown Fellow's fault," David cried wildly. "It's his old magic, so it is!"

"Well, you won your contest," said the Brown Fellow's voice from the turf sods. "You needn't complain."

"Yes, but *I* have need to complain," cried Mrs. Mc-Ivor, picking up her broken china. "I never asked you to grant my son's silly wish. How you can sit there, smoking, and see the fool he's making of himself is more than I can say."

"Maybe it'll pass off when he sleeps," said Kate hopefully.

Well, David couldn't sleep, of course, with his two arms walloping away at an imaginary drum. He wouldn't have got much to eat either if his mother hadn't managed to feed him. And the Brown Fellow chuckled and puffed at his pipe, and poor David nearly went wild—seeing the clouds of tobacco smoke, and hearing the chuckle coming from the pile of sods.

Out he went into the garden, where his sister Kate had thrown her mats over the line to beat them.

"Here, you can help me," she said, and put a pair of sticks into his hands.

It was fun beating the mats. But when David had nearly beaten them into holes, and then had beaten mats for the neighbors on both sides, he began to get tired of it.

"Mother," he wailed, going into the kitchen and knocking a jug of milk from the poor woman's hand. "Mother, what's to become of me? I can't eat or sleep and I can't work unless I set up as a mat-beater and go round the country banging mats!" And one of David's arms swept the clock and the china dogs fell from the mantelpiece to the hearth where they smashed.

Mrs. McIvor burst out crying. "And you can sit there, Brown Fellow, and see this trouble come on the family," she cried wildly.

"Well, I'm sorry, ma'am," said the Brown Fellow. "The lad brought it on himself. He was the best piccolo player in the country, and he must needs decide to be the best drummer, too. Anyway, although I know there must be a way to break this spell I can't for the life of me think of it. Memory's not what it was! But I'm thinking about it."

So he sat and puffed his pipe and a great cloud of tobacco smoke hung over the turf pile all day.

Finally, David was so tired of waving his arms that he begged his mother and Kate to get ropes and tie them to his sides. So they did, and he sat by the fire and was just nodding off to sleep when the ropes suddenly snapped and he knocked the pipe right out of the Brown Fellow's mouth and smashed it on the hearth.

"This is too much!" said the Brown Fellow angrily.

"Yes, it's too much," cried poor David. "Mother, will you fetch Peter the Blacksmith and tell him that he can take away my beautiful drum. I'll make him a present of it if he'll come and fit a strong chain around my arms so that I can't do anymore damage in the place."

"Oh, my poor boy," cried his mother. "The drum that you spent your savings on—and the shame of having Peter the Blacksmith see you like this."

"Never mind," said David. "I don't want the drum. All I want is to have quiet in my arms and to play my piccolo again. Mother, get your hat and go for the blacksmith."

Mrs. McIvor had hardly gone into the bedroom when David heard a shuffling from the corner by the turf pile, then the wheezing of an old man's breath crossed the kitchen.

"Mother," he cried. "Our Brown Fellow is leaving us! Oh, Mother, stop him! I've driven him away."

"I am *not* leaving," said the Brown Fellow, as David's mother dashed back in terror. "I'm going for some tobacco and another pipe. I'm thinking you've just about broken the spell yourself, David boy. When the blacksmith has taken your drum away he won't need to chain your arms. You'll be able to play my favorite jig for me tonight as neatly as ever you did—now that the foolish ambition to be *too* clever is gone from you."

And the Brown Fellow was right. When Peter the Blacksmith had laughed his fill and gone off with the drum, David found that the spell was broken. How gladly he seized his piccolo! He was never discontented with it again and nothing pleased him better than to play all the Brown Fellow's favorite tunes. And he never passed the turf pile without politely nodding to the little fellow that he knew was sitting there.

THE HERMIT'S

CABBAGE PATCH

———— ❀ ❀ ❀ ————

SOMEWHERE in the mountains of the West of Ireland there is a deep, round valley shaped exactly like the inside of a teacup. Very, very many years ago a hermit lived in a cave in the center of this valley. He was widely famed for the medicines which he brewed, and people came from all sides for cough cures, tonics, embrocations, and even potions to cure bad dreams, snoring, baldness, bad temper, and warts.

One warm evening Tomas Ruadh climbed up into the mountains to visit the Hermit who was working in the fine cabbage patch outside his cave. At first sight one might have taken him for a scarecrow—although no decent scarecrow would have worn his rags. But at a second glance one would have seen that out of the tangled white mop of hair and beard

)2m

RUE - AH

two very bright eyes and a long nose were peering, and both eyes and nose were very much alive. So were the bony old hands which were picking caterpillars from the cabbages and dropping them into a jar.

"God bless the work," said Tomas Ruadh. "I've seldom seen finer cabbages."

"God save you kindly," replied a voice deep within the Hermit's beard.

"I've come to you with a bit of a problem," said Tomas Ruadh.

"I can't help you," said the Hermit, and he went on picking caterpillars. "I've retired."

"It's not really myself that needs help," said Tomas Ruadh. "It's my golden-haired daughter, Brigideen."

"I'm an old man," said the Hermit. "I tell you I've retired."

"Listen," protested Tomas Ruadh. "Brigideen is promised in marriage to one of the finest and richest men in the whole country. He was passing one washday and he helped the girl to lift her tub of clothes over the ditch into the field. As he watched her spreading the linen he fell in love with her—with my beautiful golden-haired daughter!"

"Your daughter's hair is the color of a ginger cat," said the Hermit. "But, go on."

"I'm a poor man," said Tomas Ruadh. "I can give

her no dowry, but it's not that that's causing the trouble. It's the wedding dress. Brigideen won't set a day for the wedding until I can give her a dress that will be finer than any worn by the great ladies that will be at the marriage. She has her pride, that girl of mine!"

"I can't make clothes," said the Hermit crossly. "If I could I'd have made some for myself years ago. Anyway, I've retired, I tell you."

"I don't want you to make a wedding dress," said Tomas Ruadh. "I want you to brew a fertilizer for my land, so that my crops will yield twice as much, and then I'll have money to buy the dress. You can easily do that for me. Why are you so set on retiring?"

"I'm old," said the Hermit. "I make mistakes now. Listen, I had the Blacksmith from Gortmore up here, looking for a cure for the hiccups. Well, I got things mixed up and gave him a potion I had brewed which was to strengthen the growth of a man's hair."

"The blacksmith wouldn't need that," commented Tomas Ruadh. "He's known all over the country for the growth of beard he has, and the hair on his arms and chest."

"I know," said the Hermit. "That's just it. He took the hair tonic for his hiccups, and his hair grew so much that they say his wife has to clip him with the sheep shears every morning. So you see it's time I retired. I'm only fit to grow cabbages."

"You can't retire until you've helped me to buy a dress for Brigideen," said Tomas Ruadh. "When will I call back for the fertilizer?"

"All right," said the Hermit. "Your ginger-haired daughter shall have her dress. But it will take some time. I'll have to try the brew first on my own garden. Go away now, Tomas, like a decent man, and let me pick these little thieves off my cabbages while I have a leaf or two left."

For several days the Hermit boiled and brewed and steeped and mixed until he had a mess of dreadful-looking stuff, which smelled so horrible that he had to hold his long nose every time he went near it.

"There should be great growth in that," said the Hermit, and one fine morning he poured the mixture round the roots of one of his cabbage plants. "Now we'll see what happens."

He saw, and a good deal sooner than he expected. Within about ten minutes the cabbage was noticeably larger than the others, and was beginning to heart.

"I'm not so old or stupid at all," said the Hermit proudly. "Retire! Not me!" and he lay down in the sun beside the cabbages and went fast asleep.

When he awoke it seemed that it must be evening, it was so dark and cold. But no—he was lying in the shadow of a large tree. But he couldn't be under a tree? There were no trees in the valley. He walked into the open to have a better look at it, and then his heart nearly stopped beating. It was not a tree, but the cabbage, and it was still growing.

"Yes, it *is* time I retired," said the Hermit. "Not a doubt in the world about it. That brew was far too strong. Now I'll have to go down to the village and borrow an axe to cut that down. It shades the whole garden, and I simply won't have it there."

It was a long way to the village, and darkness overtook the Hermit as he climbed up the mountainside. He knew the way well, but oddly enough, in the darkness, he could not find his valley. At last he was forced to lie down in the shelter of some boulders and wait until morning.

When the light came he saw why he had been unable to find the valley. There wasn't a valley any longer. Instead, there was a shining green mound filling the valley, like an egg sitting in an eggcup. There was only one thing it could be—it was a hard head of cabbage, so ripe that the outer leaves had already dropped off, leaving it shiny, glossy, and compact.

The Hermit pushed the tangle of white hair back

from his eyes and looked again. The cabbage was still there. He went right up to the rim of the valley and kicked at the thing with his foot. And it was then that he saw the caterpillar. The caterpillar had just awakened, too. He had gone to sleep last night on a cabbage, a great big one, but still possible to eat. Now he was stranded on this huge, shiny green thing —and he couldn't get his teeth into it at all. He crawled this way and that, but he would never have managed a mouthful, had not the Hermit noticed his plight.

"You might as well have your breakfast," said the Hermit, and he broke into the side of the cabbage with his axe, and placed the caterpillar in the opening. "Now, you creature, try there where it's softer."

The caterpillar tried, and this time he began to crunch happily. It was splendid cabbage, and he could feel himself getting bigger and stronger every minute.

The Hermit was not so happy. He sat down and wondered sadly what he was to do. He could not go home to his cave because the cabbage completely blocked the valley. He could not go back to the village because the people would laugh at him and say he was mad. He envied the caterpillar, who seemed to be having the time of his life. The crunching was getting louder and louder.

The Hermit's Cabbage Patch

The Hermit turned round, and his eyes nearly popped out of his head. The caterpillar was now at least six feet long, and he was eating as if he intended to go on forever.

"It's a strange world," said the Hermit. "A ginger-haired girl wants a wedding dress, and this is what comes of it. It's certainly a most extraordinary world!"

The more the caterpillar ate the larger it grew, and its mouthfuls became bigger and bigger. By the time another day and night had passed the cabbage wasn't like an egg in a cup any more. It was like an empty eggshell, with a simply monstrous caterpillar crunching away at the remains. The poor Hermit cowered on the edge of the valley, which looked like a valley again, but every time the monster inside raised its head, he went scurrying down the hillside, shaking with terror.

"I'll never be able to fancy a bite of cabbage again," he said sadly. "Not even spring cabbage, or white cabbage boiled in with a bit of bacon."

But everything that had grown from the Hermit's fertilizer had developed in far less than the normal time. Next day the valley was silent and apparently empty. Not a scrap of cabbage remained, except a huge stump, like the trunk of a tree. The Hermit decided that the monster had gone off to look for more food, and with his axe in his hand he crept very cautiously down into the valley. Not a sign of the caterpillar! He reached the mouth of his cave and peeped in. The whole cave was blocked with soft white stuff, like cotton wool.

"So he has used my cave to spin himself a cocoon," said the Hermit. "At the rate things are going he should have turned into a butterfly by tomorrow or the next day. I'll just have to wait!" And he sat down beside the cabbage stalk and waited.

Next day a huge white butterfly crawled out of the cave, and the Hermit was able to clear the mess out of his cave and move in again himself. The big butterfly flew a few times round the valley and then came back to the Hermit. It wanted to make friends. It felt lonely, and the flowers in the valley were too small to feed it with honey.

The Hermit filled his big cauldron with sugar and water and the butterfly sipped happily, and then perched on the cabbage stump and folded his glorious wings.

"You are truly a beautiful thing," said the Hermit. "What a pity a butterfly lives such a short time."

And on the very next day the great butterfly died.

"So ends my last attempt to brew anything," said the Hermit. "This time I really *have* retired."

But that evening Tomas Ruadh visited him again.

"Where's my fertilizer?" he demanded. "Have you forgotten about my child's dress? My beautiful, golden-haired daughter, who will be a lady when she marries!"

"Forgotten?" screamed the Hermit. "I've had a dreadful time on account of your daughter—who has ginger hair and a face as plain as a milk pudding! But—but—the child's not to blame. She is a good girl, and a plain bride deserves the best wedding gown. Just wait a minute!" And the Hermit hurried into his cave, and came out with his arms full of something soft, velvety, and pure white. The wings of the great butterfly.

"Here, Tomas Ruadh," he said. "Don't crush it. Tell Brigideen to make her dress, and she'll look like a princess. Go off now, Tomas, and tell everybody that I've *retired*, gone out of business, broken my mixing bowls and bottles, and that I'll never mix another brew as long as I live."

This time he kept his word. He worked in his little garden, but he never dared to grow another cabbage. He grew carrots, for he said they reminded him that he had given a red-haired girl the finest wedding dress ever to be seen in Ireland.